W9-ATG-073

DISCARD

NOV   2005

The
Jesse Tree

For my mother and father G.M.

To the tree, with gratitude B.W.

The
Jesse Tree

GERALDINE MCCAUGHREAN

Illustrated by BEE WILLEY

EERDMANS BOOKS FOR YOUNG READERS

Grand Rapids, Michigan • Cambridge, U.K.

Text copyright © 2003 Geraldine McCaughrean
Illustrations copyright © 2003 Bee Willey
The Jesse Tree copyright © 2003 Lion Publishing

First published in Great Britin in 2003 by
Lion Publishing plc
Mayfield House, 256 Banbury Road,
Oxford OX2 7DH, England
www.lion-publishing.co.uk

This edition published in 2005 under license from Lion Publishing
by Eerdmans Books for Young Readers
an imprint of Wm. B. Eerdmans Publishing Co.,
255 Jefferson SE, Grand Rapids, Michigan 49503
P.O. Box 163, Cambridge CB39PU U.K.

05 06 07 08 09 10 11 7 6 5 4 3 2 1

Library of Congress Cataloging-in-Publication Data

McCaughrean, Geraldine.
The Jesse tree / written by Geraldine McCaughrean ; illustrated by Bee Willey.
p. cm.
Summary: The stories that tell of Christ's lineage unfold as an old carpenter begrudgingly tells a young boy about the
Jesse tree he is carving.

ISBN 0-8028-5288-2 (alk. paper)

[1. Jesse trees--Fiction. 2. Jesus Christ--Fiction. 3. Carpentry--Fiction.] I. Willey, Bee, ill. II. Title.
PZ7.M4784133Je 2005
[Fic]--dc22
2004020227

Typeset in 13/18 Elegant Garamond BT
Printed and bound in India

CONTENTS

INTRODUCTION

In the old days, in the front of any family Bible, a record was kept of that family's history: the marriages, the children born of those marriages, the marriages and offspring of those children. Over the course of generations, those fading, spidery lines spread outwards, like branches and twigs from a single trunk. That is why we call such a record a "family tree."

Similarly, there would have been, in any number of churches, a "Jesse tree" — a depiction of Jesus' family tree in wood, or stone, or stained glass. Church garments might even have been embroidered with a tree.

Even thousands of years ago, when the stories of the Old Testament were first told, families were pictured as trees branching out from a single trunk.

"A shoot will spring from the stock of Jesse, and from his roots a bud will blossom," said the prophet Isaiah in the Bible, foretelling the birth of Jesus. It is this verse which gave rise to the tradition of Jesse trees in churches.

Jesse trees were the Bible-storybooks of unlettered people. A priest could point to the figures or symbols and tell the stories of those Old Testament kings, prophets, heroines, warriors. And the tree itself served to show how the New Testament grew out of the Old Testament; how, for Christians, the birth of Jesus was not just a beginning, but a completion. He was the flowering of a tree planted long before, by God's own design. By tracing his earthly ancestry back to King David and beyond, it was easy, too, to see Jesus as a real historical figure.

That forest of ancient Jesse trees fashioned in the Middle Ages is long gone. Puritan vandals of the seventeenth century, in their attempt to destroy all "graven images," smashed the heads from saints, the wings from angels, the figures from Jesse trees. No tree survives undamaged.

But in recent times, a new tradition has grown up — a new strain of Jesse tree "grown" at home. Still planted for the sake of its stories, symbols are added day by day during the season of Advent, and day by day the old stories are retold, culminating in the stories of the first Christmas.

Whether you read the twenty-four stories in this book during Advent or enjoy it at one sitting in the shade of a summer tree, remember that the Jesse tree's roots were put down centuries ago, and that its fruit is as sweet as ever.

THE JESSE TREE

"What are you doing, mister?"

The old carpenter frowned. He hated people to watch him work. The big silence of the empty church suited him very well. When he saw the boy standing there, his frown turned to a scowl.

"What are you doing in here?" he growled.

"I asked first."

The old man ran a creased hand over his half-completed woodwork. "I'm carving a Jesse tree, if you must know. Now run along out of here. A church isn't for playing in."

"Is that your name then? Jesse?"

The carpenter was impatient to get back to work. "Of course not. A Jesse tree is a very ancient tradition. A thousand years ago, every church had a Jesse tree. A stained-glass window or a carved wooden screen . . . Nowadays, it's a lost art."

"No, it's not," said the boy. "You're doing it."

He wore a tee shirt and shorts: a tourist, thought the old man with disgust. Vacationers! They came to town, they made a mess, made a nuisance, then away they went. Small boys on vacation were the worst.

"Why a tree?" asked the boy.

The carpenter breathed out through his teeth. "It's like a family tree. You've heard of a family tree? Well, a Jesse tree is like that. It shows the ancestors of Jesus Christ, from the start of the world until his birth. You've heard of Jesus, I suppose?"

"I've heard of Jesus. Were the sun and moon his ancestors, then?" asked the boy, pointing to the carvings near the base of the tree.

"Of course not," snapped the old man. "Those are symbols. They mark the start of the story. The beginning."

"I like stories," said the boy.

"Go and watch TV, then."

But the boy did not go. He sat down on a pew. "Have you forgotten the story?"

he asked after a moment.

"Huh! You should know it already, ignorant child. When I was your age, we knew all the stories in the Bible. These days . . ."

"So tell me," said the boy.

And there was nothing for the carpenter to do but to tell the boy the story behind the carvings of the sun and moon.

PARADISE GARDEN

First there was the idea, complete and perfect: the beginning, the end, and everything in between. (God is a craftsman, you see, and a craftsman always plans before he begins work.) Then God flexed his fingers and began. He made light and with it warmth and beauty (because you can't see beauty in the dark). He took all the makings in his two palms — energy, gases, liquids, and solids — and when he had finished, there was the world, spinning in and out of sunlight, with the moon to light the dark hours.

He put fish in the seas and animals on land and, in the loveliest spot of all, he planted a garden. Last of all, he made a gardener — out of clay — prettier than a sloth, not as marvelous as an angel; somewhere between the two. That was Adam, the first man.

To keep Adam from being lonely, God took one of Adam's ribs, and from it he made Eve, the first woman—smoother, softer, smaller. But in one special way, Adam and Eve were not like the other animals. When God breathed life into them, he passed on a little something of himself.

———————

"A family likeness, you mean. I get you. My mom says I look like my grandma," said the boy. "But why the sun and moon? Why didn't you carve Adam and Eve?"

"I told you, boy. These are symbols. They represent the time when God began his great plan. As it happens, Adam and Eve almost ruined everything . . . But people who come into this church will look at this sun, this moon, and remember how God created the world."

"And now you are creating it all over again," said the boy.

The old man was so angry that his fist tightened around his chisel and he shook it. "Don't talk wickedness, boy! I don't liken myself to God! That'd be falling into the sin of pride, that would!"

The boy looked startled. "Why? You said it yourself: there's a likeness. A family likeness. It's just that you're using wood, not clay. Go on with the story."

"I'm not here to tell stories!" raged the old man. "I'm here to work — if I'm left in peace."

"Is that what Adam and Eve did? Stop God working? You said they nearly ruined everything. What did they do?"

The old man felt cornered, as if a dog had pinned him against the wall of the great empty church. He looked towards the door for a mother or father who might come and call the boy off. No such luck.

———————

"There is everything here in Paradise Garden that you will ever need," said God to Adam and Eve. "Food, shelter, birdsong. Me. Eat whatever you want — strawberries, mangoes, honey, anything. Just don't eat from the tree in the middle of the garden — the tree of knowledge."

It was a test, you see; a test of their love for God.

Suddenly, of course, there was nothing so interesting to Adam and Eve as that tree in the middle of the garden. Why was this one different from the rest? How? Time and again, Adam and Eve were drawn back to stare at the forbidden fruit of the tree of knowledge.

"Eat," said a voice to Eve. "Taste and then you will know. Why else is it called the tree of knowledge?" A beautiful creature with shimmering scales and a forked tongue crept out from among the roots. "Eat. Then you will know as much as God himself."

It was a test, you see, of whether they would put themselves or God first. With a delicious shudder of excitement, Eve picked a juicy piece of fruit and bit into it. Adam ate too. Bitter. No great wisdom descended on them. All they knew was that they should not have done it. They looked down, and their slender brown bodies didn't look beautiful anymore. "Now look what you've done, woman! Cover yourself up!" snapped Adam.

"You too! You too!" Eve complained.

God knew at once, of course. They could hide among the bushes, stitch clothing out of leaves, but God knew. Suddenly the birds in Paradise Garden sang out of key.

"Why did you disobey me?" God asked sadly. "Now you will have to go. The garden can no longer offer you a home. Don't come back until you have found my forgiveness."

So Adam and Eve were driven out of the garden and began a long, hard journey that lasted all their lives and much, much longer. Their children and their children's children went looking for the way back to Paradise Garden, but none of them could find it. They all disobeyed God, too — some in much worse ways than Adam and Eve's. Much worse. God had a rescue plan, of course. One day he planned to send . . ."

"So what happened to the garden?" the boy interrupted.

The question took the old man by surprise. "God set an angel at the gate with a fiery sword — *to keep out trespassers*," he added pointedly.

"But what happened to the tree of knowledge? Did God chop it down?"

This was insufferable. "I don't know! Maybe. Why should he? It's lost to us, at any rate. You and I will never see it."

The boy got up and came closer to examine the knobbly roots of the carved Jesse tree. "That's why you are planting a new one."

The old carpenter grunted his disgust. "Haven't you been listening to a word I said? I told you — this is a *Jesse* tree, not the tree of knowledge."

"It's teaching *me* plenty," said the boy.

Then he was gone.

A BOAT FULL OF ANIMALS

"Get it out! Get it out!"

Startled by the shout, the wet dog standing beside the boy began to bark. The noise rang round the church.

"What are you thinking, bringing an animal into the church?"

"It's raining," said the boy. The dog shook itself and water drops spattered them both. "Don't you like dogs?"

"Isn't it bad enough to have bugs eating away at the roof without having wet dogs, too?"

"I like boats," interrupted the boy.

The carpenter scowled down at his latest carving. "It's not a boat, you ignorant child. It's an ark."

"It has no sails. How did it go?"

"It didn't have to go. All it had to do was float."

The dog suddenly lay down, like a collapsing sandcastle, its eyes glistening and its ears cocked. Now two of them wanted a story!

Too many boys making a nuisance of themselves. I expect that was half the trouble . . . As the world filled up with the sons and granddaughters and great-great-great-grandchildren of Adam and Eve, it got worse instead of better. In fact, God decided he had been wrong to create the human race at all. The earth crawled with wickedness — like when the flying ants swarm.

Noah was different. A good man. He kept his tools clean, kept his conscience clear. God liked Noah.

"Noah," said God. "A flood is coming. It will wash away every living thing — wash the earth clean again. But you and your family are my friends: I wish you no harm. Do exactly as I say . . ."

Now, this was a dry, hot part of the world, a long way from the sea. When Noah's neighbors saw him building a ship, they snickered and held out their palms and squinted at the sky. "What's the ship for, Noah? Expecting rain? Tee-hee." Noah's ark was huge, with three decks and a roof over all.

"Why so big, Noah? Expecting visitors?" snorted the neighbors and scrawled on the hull with lumps of chalk.

Then the animals started to come: lions and lynxes and leopards. The neighbors stayed away after that. There were warm-blooded and cold-skinned beasts, furry and feathered, smooth and scaly. There were crawlers and leapers, grazers and scavengers, wild and tame. There were creatures with names and ones so odd that only God knew what they were called. Inside the ark, they shifted, whined and gibbered. There were males and there were females: one of each. There were butterflies and even birds.

"Why birds, God?" wondered Noah. "Surely birds can fly into the treetops when the flood comes."

But when the flood came, there were no treetops. Rain fell from the sky like a waterfall, uprooting trees and boulders and towns. Noah's wife and family went aboard the ark and shut the doors. The darkness inside was warm with animals, sweet with animal breath. Things skittered unseen across the floor. Rain thudded on the roof.

The neighbors beat on the hull. "Let us in!"

The rivers filled, burst, joined. The distant sea came ashore. The ark grated, rolled, pitched, spun, and was washed away like a coconut carried out to sea. Inside the ark, the animals blinked at Noah. The drumming of the rain wiped out every other sound.

The tarry planks kept out the daylight. Aboard the ark, day and night were the same color. The animals slept and woke. The smell was soon as thick as mud.

Only after forty days and forty nights did the rain stop. But when Noah lifted off the hatches, he saw only sun and sky and water. There were no treetops — not even any mountaintops. Litter floated by: a shoe, a basket, a wooden spoon.

The wet ark steamed. The water dimpled. Bubbles rose. A fish jumped: the only sign of life. It was the beginning of the world again. Somewhere in the ark, a blackbird started to sing.

Weeks passed. The ark stank. The elephants swayed listlessly from foot to foot. Now, surely, the flood must be drying up.

"Fetch me a raven," said Noah.

The raven cruised out over the water, its reflection like a black fish. But it found nowhere to land.

Next, Noah sent a dove. But after a while it returned; it had found the world still underwater. Seven days later, Noah sent the dove out again. When it came back, it held in its beak a tiny olive twig. Somewhere, an olive tree must be poking its branches through the shining water! Next time Noah loosed the dove, it did not come back at all.

With a grinding shudder, the ark ran aground on a mountaintop. The animals growled and bellowed, squealed and chattered and spat. Noah's daughter-in-law stroked her round stomach; her baby would after all be born on dry land. New life in a new world. The water and the sky and the breeze and the light whispered, "Never again!"

Mud squelched under the hooves of a horse that picked its way across the sodden ground. "Now we must get things right," said Noah, "or next time . . ."

Suddenly, it was as if the sky remembered color. A great triumphal arch of streaming color bridged the sky from horizon to horizon. "Never again," whispered God. "Never again will I drown the earth," and he signed his promise with the world's first rainbow.

The rain had stopped. Sunlight streamed through the stained-glass windows and cast a rainbow over the wet dog. "So, Noah must be Jesus' ancestor, right? Because there was no one else left after the flood?"

"That's what some people say," muttered the carpenter.

"So Noah must be your ancestor, too, come to that. And mine. That makes us relatives!"

"Oh, now, wait a moment . . ."

"Did people do better the second time around?" asked the boy.

"Not so you'd notice," grunted the carpenter, and went back to carving the waves beneath his oaken ark.

"Was that God's rescue plan, then?" asked the boy. "You said he had a rescue plan. Bit drastic. Wipe everybody out and start again."

"No, no! Well, yes, but no." The carpenter looked confused. "In the long run, God was planning to send Jesus. That's the rescue plan I was talking about. . ."

But the boy was busy with his own thoughts. "Were there bugs on the ark, do you think?"

"Definitely not! Perishing little pests!"

"There must've been. Or they wouldn't be here now," said the boy.

"Get that dog out of here and don't bring it back! I don't know what things are coming to! Dogs in the Lord's house, indeed!"

STRANGE VISITORS

There was no dog with the boy when he came the next day. There was a little boy instead.

"You mean there are more of you?" said the old man with a despairing sigh.

"He was lost. I said I'd show him the way back to the campground." He turned to the smaller boy. "There's the Jesse tree I told you about. There's the sun and moon, there's the boat, and now he's doing a horse."

"It's not a horse. It's a camel," snapped the carpenter.

"Did it get left behind by Noah? Is it wading? It's got no legs."

"It's sitting down. Resting in the desert. It stands for . . . I mean, it's a symbol for Abraham."

"Was Abraham a camel, then?"

The old man scowled such a scowl that both boys ought to have melted then and there. But they didn't. "Sit down," the boy advised his friend. "He's going to tell us the story of Abraham now."

Abraham was a nomad; he did not belong anywhere. His tent was like the ark floating on the flood — one day here, another day there. When the goats and sheep had eaten all the grass in one place, Abraham and his wife, Sarah, moved on. They did not mind. God was good to them. The only regret they had was their lack of a son. Year after year they had longed for a child. Too many years. Now Sarah was too old. It seemed that, when Abraham and Sarah died, their tent and sheep and camels would pass to strangers.

———————————

"Yes? Go on," said the boy. "Why did you stop?"

"I never meant to start," said the old man gruffly, polishing his chisel on the tail of his shirt. But he went on.

———————————

Then one day, three figures walked out of the low light. The heat made their shapes waver.

Sarah was inside the tent, preparing food, but Abraham beckoned to them. "Come! Eat! Drink! Rest, strangers!"

"You are a hospitable man, Abraham. May your son bring you great joy. Children do."

"We have no child," said Abraham. "My wife, Sarah . . ."

". . . will have a son," one stranger interrupted. "And that son will be the father of many sons."

Inside the tent, Sarah heard this and laughed to herself: a soft, bitter, inward laugh.

"Why did Sarah laugh?" asked another of the strangers. "Doesn't she know that with God all things are possible?"

The tent trembled, and suddenly Sarah stood in its doorway, staring. They could not possibly have heard her laugh! How could they know a thing like that? How could they? A group of strangers . . .

The visitors drank goat's milk, broke bread with Abraham, and walked on. The desert dust swallowed them up. The heat broke the setting sun into white crumbs of light. The first star of evening was rising.

"Can you believe it?" gasped Sarah, half-laughing, her hand resting on her stomach.

"I can," said Abraham. "I do. I've told you before how God spoke to me once — years ago — and said, 'Abraham, your descendants will be as numberless as the stars in the sky.' I should not have needed three strangers to tell me. I should have known: God always keeps his promises."

———————————

"And Abraham is one of Jesus' ancestors, right, and that's why you're carving his camel on the Jesse tree?"

"Correct."

"So Jesus was going to be one of Abraham's many, many, many, many countless-as-the-stars descendants, right?" said the boy.

"Yes, yes." The old man tossed his head irritably, as if these things were too complicated for boys to understand.

"The brightest one."

"Yes, yes. The brightest one. Can a working man get no peace these days?"

A TEST OF LOVE

"This is my little brother. He cut himself." The voice was all too familiar to the carpenter, who gave a glum sigh. "I took him to the first aid station on the beach. But I thought you could cheer him up with a story. The sheep's new."

"It's a ram," said the old man, running a rough palm over his latest carving.

The little brother curled up on a pew to listen.

———————

When Sarah gave birth to a son — (oh yes, God kept his promise) — Abraham called him Isaac, which means "he laughed." The child must have taken after his mother, you see. Isaac was a fine boy — not like some you see nowadays. He was helpful to his mother, did as he was told, was good with the animals, and was brave and handsome and clever. To Abraham and Sarah, he seemed even more special, because they had waited so long for him. That is what made it all the harder . . .

The morning was cold, but there were beads of sweat on Abraham's neck as he lashed a bundle of firewood to the donkey's back. "Fetch me a big knife, Isaac, and a coil of rope. We have to go into the mountains and offer a sacrifice to God."

It was not unusual. In those days, people often made burnt offerings on their altars: the first sheaf of harvest, the best lamb from the flock. It was a way of thanking God for his goodness.

"Where are you going, Abraham?" said Sarah, snatching at his arm. "Why is your face so pale?" But Abraham would not answer. The donkey seemed unwilling to move. It leaned back against the bridle.

But at last they were on their way up the mountain paths — Isaac carrying a lighted torch, Abraham tugging the donkey along.

"Oh! Have we forgotten the lamb for the sacrifice?" asked Isaac, hoping they would not have to turn back.

"God will provide that," said Abraham. His face was as empty as a broken jug. They did not talk after that.

The highest places are the holiest. Abraham climbed up very high indeed. Then he piled up the firewood, turned awkwardly and wrapped his arms round his son. It was something between a hug and a grab. "Son, it's you! God wants you for the sacrifice!"

No laughter now from Isaac.

Abraham bound him with the rope, and laid him on the altar. The knife in one hand, he placed the other over his son's face — over his eyes. His fist rose to make the blow. Quickly now, quickly. Get it over. Done. Get it done . . . The tears in his eyes made rainbows of everything . . .

"Abraham! Abraham!" The voice came from nowhere and from everywhere. "Stop! Enough. Look."

A nearby thorn bush shook. An animal bleated. A ram had tangled its horns in the bush and couldn't get free. Together father and son dragged it to the altar and offered it up to God. Its blood stained them both.

It had been a test, you see, to prove whether there was anything or anyone Abraham loved more than God; whether there was anything he would try to keep back from God.

"But you've carved the ram — not Abraham or Isaac. People might think Jesus was descended from a sheep. You know, the one that had to die."

"Don't be ridiculous."

The little brother had fallen asleep along the pew, his cut hand folded across his chest. They both stood looking down at him.

"I couldn't," said the boy. "Could you?"

"Could I what?"

"Pass the test. Kill your son."

Suddenly the angry carpenter was brandishing his chisel, high up over their heads, for all the world like a big knife. *"I don't have a son!"*

"Oh," said the boy, unperturbed. "Maybe that's why you don't laugh much."

After they were gone, the old man returned, grumbling, to his work.

But the words kept chipping at his brain, in time with the tapping of his mallet. The sheep that had to die. Jesus: the sheep that had to die.

STAIRWAY TO HEAVEN

"I had a dream last night."

The old man jumped. Could the boy not cough politely or say, "Excuse me?" Must he just suddenly be there, talking? It scattered the old man's thoughts like birds out of a tree.

"I dreamed I was Jack, climbing the beanstalk."

"I only have nightmares," said the carpenter.

"Was one of Jesus' ancestors a firefighter?"

"Certainly not . . . why?"

"Well, where's that ladder going?" He came and put his small fingers on the rungs of the ladder that stood propped mysteriously among the leaves of the carved Jesse tree.

"Don't meddle," said its maker.

The little fingers climbed the ladder, rung by rung. "Tell me."

———————————

Everything about Jacob was smooth, from his well-washed skin to the words in his mouth. Only his wits were sharp. His mother thought the world of him. His father, Isaac, preferred Esau, though. Esau was rough and tough, as different as straw from silk — and Esau was his firstborn son.

Esau and Jacob were twins, born only moments apart, but in those days it mattered very much who came first into the light of day. So Esau was his father's heir and Jacob wasn't. When Isaac died, Esau would become head of the family and Jacob wouldn't. That one thought chafed, like straw against silk.

Esau was a hunter, forever chasing deer across the plains and through the tangled woods. Jacob preferred to stay at home. His mother liked to have him near her. Also he had plenty of time to think.

One day, Esau came home half-dead with weariness. He flung himself down, muddy from head to foot and with twigs in his hair. "Give me something to eat, brother. I'm exhausted."

Quietly, Jacob glided to the fire and filled a wooden bowl with stew. Its scent filled the room, rich and delicious. "You give me your birthright," he said teasingly, "and I'll give you the stew."

"Hurry up. I'm starving to death," complained Esau.

"It's yours . . . in return for your birthright."

"What do you mean, my birthright? Give me the stew, can't you?"

"From now on, I'm the firstborn. That's all."

Esau wagged a weary hand. "Whatever you say." After all, how could a bowl of stew change the facts? Esau had seen the light of day first. He wolfed down the stew and fell fast asleep.

But Jacob held him to the deal. By the time Esau woke, everyone knew that he had sold his place as Isaac's heir in return for a bowl of stew. His only comfort? He was still his father's favorite son. His father's blessing would surely come to him.

"Hunt a deer and cook its meat for me," whispered old Isaac one day, frail as a cobweb, as blind and chilly as ice. "Then I shall give you my dying blessing."

Now, in those days, a father's blessing was considered as powerful as a wish granted. Away went Esau to catch his deer. In slid Jacob, subtle as a cat, his forearms covered in strips of fur, his borrowed clothes smelling of the woods. (His mother had put him up to it.)

"Here you are, Father. It's me, Esau. I brought you the venison you asked for."

Isaac took the bowl of tender meat from Jacob — as unsuspecting as Esau had been when he had taken the stew.

"My boy," the old man said, feeling the coarse, hairy hands that clasped the bowl. "Let me kiss you. My blessing is yours." And thus, for a second time, Jacob stole from his brother.

When Esau found out how he had been cheated, he begged Isaac to bless him too.

"My blessing is given," said the old man, sharing his son's sorrow.

Esau was so angry that Jacob had to run for his life — out into the countryside where he had never hunted, out into the woods where the deer knew the way better than he did, out under a scowling sky. Who knows why God forgave Jacob — the trickster, the cheat — except that God forgives most things. Who knows why God leaned out of heaven and kissed Jacob on his smooth forehead? But he did.

That night, Jacob lay down to sleep, with only a rock for a pillow, and he had the strangest dream of his life.

He dreamed he saw a bright hole in the sky above him—as if he were lying on the bottom of a frozen lake, looking up through a hole in the ice. And stretching down from the hole was a ladder—the longest ladder imaginable, and as broad as a flight of stairs. Figures of snowy brightness were climbing the ladder, their faces brushed by the hems of yet more figures climbing down from above.

Angels.

"Jacob," said a voice within his dream. "Just as I promised your grandfather, Abraham, I am going to make you the father of a great people, and bring them into a land of their own."

Even when Jacob woke, the dream lingered behind in his eyelids, like a flash of lightning. He knew that God had spoken to him. He knew that being a part of God's plan would cost him more than a bowl of stew or a dish of meat. He knew that God would ask more from him than tricks and a quick wit. He was filled with excitement and joy and terror and shock, all at once.

Above all, he longed to tell his twin brother . . . but of course, that was out of the question. One day, he would have to put things right with Esau.

———————————

"I suppose, if your Jesse tree were tall enough, the angels could glide up and down that," said the boy.

"Don't talk crazy," said the old man.

But, funnily enough, that night the carpenter dreamed that his Jesse tree had grown like some magic beanstalk all the way up into the sky and that tourists were climbing up and down it, their mouths white with ice cream and laughter.

THE DREAMER

"You've been fighting!" exclaimed the carpenter the next day, when the boy came into the church. "Typical!"

"My brother wanted my baseball cap. So he took it. He's bigger than me . . . But I got it back!"

"I'll bet you did. Tit for tat. Knock for knock. That's all you kids understand these days . . ."

"I was going to bring him here. But after he took my cap, I didn't. So he won't get to hear the story, will he?"

"What story?"

"The one about that bathrobe," said the boy, pointing.

"It's not a bathrobe," protested the carpenter hotly, in defense of his latest carving. "It's Joseph's coat of many colors!"

Jacob married and had twelve sons. Twelve! The eleventh — young Joseph — was a delightful boy. At least, Jacob thought so.

Joseph was a dreamer — not a daydreamer but a night-dreamer who remembered his dreams when he woke. "Last night I dreamed we were harvesting, and your sheaves of wheat bowed down to my sheaf," he told his eleven brothers. His brothers did not think much of his dream.

"Last night I dreamed we were all stars in the sky and that you eleven stars all bowed down to me." Joseph's brothers did not want to hear this either.

"Look what Father gave me!" said Joseph one day, wagging the sleeves of a glorious new coat. "Look at all the colors! Look at the cloth!"

Joseph's brothers did not want to look. No father shouldn't love one son more than all the rest — or if he does, he shouldn't let it show. They hated Joseph for his coat and his dreams and his unfair share of love.

So one day, when Joseph brought them their lunch — way out in the hills, out of sight of home — they grabbed him, tore off the fancy coat and threw him into a pit.

Like a crumpled rainbow the coat was laid at old Jacob's feet. "A terrible accident, Father!" they said. "Dear little Joseph . . . Some wild animal must have . . . All we found was this . . . He must be dead." Then the grief in Jacob's eyes made their lies peter out to a sorry silence.

But Joseph was not dead. Even hating him the way they did, his brothers had stopped short of murder. They had gone back to the pit, arguing about what to do with him. As they argued, a caravan of camels clanked by, bound for Egypt. "Let's sell him for a slave!" suggested Judah. And they watched their hated brother be led away, stumbling, dirt-colored, in the dust behind the camel train.

Suddenly, realizing what a long story he had begun, the carpenter pulled himself up short. "I haven't got time for this! I've got work to do."

"All right. I'll come back tomorrow for the rest. But promise . . ."

"Promise? I don't have to pro —"

" . . . if my big brother comes by, don't tell him that story. It might give him ideas."

FAMINE AND PLENTY

"I suppose he came back?" said a voice the next day. "It wouldn't be much of a story if Joseph . . ."

"Much of a story? Much of a story? The Bible wasn't written to entertain you, you know!" The chisel trembled in the leathery old hands. "And no, Joseph didn't come back. He stayed in Egypt. He had a gift, didn't he? God had given him a gift. Joseph understood dreams — not his own, maybe, but other people's dreams."

In Egypt, things went from bad to worse. Although Joseph worked hard, he ended up in prison, convicted of a crime he had not committed. He felt hopeless and lost. But in Egypt, people valued dreams and dreaming. When his fellow prisoners had nightmares, Joseph explained what the dreams meant, and he was always right. The prisoners were astounded, but they forgot Joseph, of course, the moment the sunlight shone in their eyes again.

Luckily, when the pharaoh — the ruler of the country — was himself plagued with dreams that none of his advisors could interpret, someone remembered the Hebrew slave rotting in the city jail. "Send for him!" said Pharaoh, black-eyed for want of sleep.

"You dreamed of cattle clambering out of the Nile," said Joseph, as he knelt before the throne. "First seven sleek, fat cows, then seven bony, thin ones. The thin cows opened their mouths and swallowed up the fat ones."

Pharaoh flinched from the memory of his dream. "But what does it mean? Can you tell me that, Hebrew?"

"For seven years, Egypt's harvest will be marvelous — the granaries full of grain. But for seven years after that, every harvest will fail and your people will go hungry — unless you take steps to prevent it."

So impressed was Pharaoh, so taken with this dream-reader, that he made Joseph governor of Egypt. From then on, Joseph spoke on the pharaoh's behalf and was almost as powerful as the pharaoh himself.

The dreams had come from God, of course. So too did the seven years of plenty. Joseph gave orders for all the surplus food to be stored in great granaries and for nothing to go to waste. Sure enough, there followed seven years of famine, but, thanks to Joseph's careful planning, no one in Egypt starved.

Far away in Joseph's homeland, the sheep shook on their thin legs. The brothers' stomachs were empty. "Go into Egypt where the granaries are full," said their father, Jacob, "and buy grain." (His old face, drooping like the wax from a candle, had not smiled since the day they brought him Joseph's multicolored coat stained with blood.)

So that is how Joseph came to see his brothers again — they were kneeling in his chamber of state, asking permission to buy grain from the great Egyptian granaries. They did not recognize him, of course. He wore Egyptian robes, an Egyptian wig; his eyes were black-rimmed with Egyptian kohl. Besides, twenty years had passed since the business of the coat, the pit, the merchant caravan . . . But Joseph knew his brothers, oh yes, all ten of them . . .

Ten? Where was the eleventh? Where was little Benjamin, the youngest?

Joseph questioned them, demanded to know why one brother had stayed behind. To their dismay, he sent them home to fetch Benjamin. "But our father!" they protested. "He relies on Benjamin! His whole life is bound up in the boy. If anything were to happen . . ." They might as well have been talking to the pyramids themselves. Joseph was adamant.

So Benjamin was fetched, and the brothers were allowed to load their pack animals with good grain and to set off, marveling at the generosity of that governor of Egypt, marveling at the splendor of the Egyptian civilization.

Then the soldiers came after them, stopped them and began to search for stolen goods. "We took nothing! On our lives, nothing!" protested the brothers. "If you find anything on one of us, let the culprit be put to death!" How they must have regretted those words when the guards reached into Benjamin's saddlebag and pulled out the silver cup and brandished it in their faces. "Not Benjamin! Benjamin would never . . ." Their hands fell helpless by their sides. Their knees failed under them.

Joseph, who had given orders for the silver cup to be planted among their belongings, looked on with grim satisfaction. His brothers were as afraid now as Joseph had been twenty years before when, wrists tied, he had stumbled into slavery behind the merchant camel train. Childhood dreams swam before Joseph's eyes — their sheaves of corn flattened before his own; their stars dimmed by his brilliance. And Joseph went into a side room and wept — for all the lost years, for all the broken dreams, for the marvelous and confusing ways in which God worked out his plan.

When Joseph revealed his true identity to his brothers, there were no reproaches, no apologies, only tears of joy and relief and healing. Jacob was sent for — a frail old man rattling his weary bones over dusty roads to be reunited with the son he had thought dead for twenty years.

And Jacob's family was not alone in finding a new home in a new country. Many more Hebrews traveled to Egypt to escape famine and stayed on there as settlers along the fertile Nile River. God had promised to take care of them, and perhaps this move to Egypt was his way of doing it. Let the Egyptians worship their boatload of animal-headed gods; the Hebrews would stay loyal to their one God. After all, they were his chosen people — his favored sons and daughters. Surely they were the ones to whom he would give the best gifts, the ones he could not help but love the best.

———————————

"You say that as if it turned out different," said the boy.

"It did," said the carpenter. "Within a few generations, life in Egypt went horribly wrong for the Hebrews."

"So God broke his promise?"

"He never promised life would be easy, only that he would stay close to his people — the children of Israel."

"You can tell me tomorrow."

The old man gave an irritable groan. As the church door slammed shut behind his visitor, he called after him, "No promises!" but probably too late to be heard.

"LET MY PEOPLE GO!"

"So what went wrong in Egypt?" It was a small voice, but it filled the big church. The boy came and stood at his elbow. "I'm hungry. The ice cream truck didn't come today. Is that a whip you're carving? Did one of Jesus' ancestors drive a stagecoach?"

"I am carving a whip to symbolize the time when the Hebrews — the Israelites, that is — were slaves. As the years passed, Joseph and the famine were forgotten.

"A new pharaoh was in power. Then the Egyptians suddenly looked around at the huge number of Hebrews living in Egypt and became afraid. So they made the Hebrew settlers their slaves and worked them like pack animals or farm beasts."

"But God had a rescue plan, I'll bet."

"Naturally."

"Jesus!"

"Noooo, no no no no! Ignorant boy. This was long, long before Jesus. This time, God saw that his chosen people were in trouble and he sent Moses."

"Did he help them escape? Tell me!"

———————

Moses could not believe his eyes. A bush was burning — and yet it was not. It looked like extra leaves grew on the twigs, yellow and red flames covered the bush but did not destroy it. Then, strangest of all, a voice spoke out of the bush: "Take off your shoes, Moses. You are standing on holy ground."

Moses shuffled out of his sandals, never once taking his eyes off the burning bush.

"I am the God of your ancestors, the God of Abraham, Isaac, and Jacob. I have heard the voice of the children of Israel crying out to me for help. So go to Egypt, Moses, and tell the pharaoh to let my people go."

These were not words Moses wanted to hear. Oh, he was an Israelite himself, and he knew very well what they were suffering. He had grown up in Egypt — not as a slave but in the pharaoh's own palace, adopted by the pharaoh's daughter. Just once he had stood up for his fellow countrymen — he had killed an overseer who was beating a Hebrew slave to death with a whip. For that, Moses had had to flee from Egypt as a hunted criminal.

"I can't. I'm sorry. You're asking the wrong —"

"You shall. I have chosen you to speak for them and to fetch my people out of slavery. Find your brother, Aaron, and take him with you if you feel the need of his eloquence. I shall be with you both. Go."

So Moses gave up his safe little life tending sheep and went back to Egypt where his fellow Israelites toiled all day under Egyptian whips.

"The God of Israel says, 'Let my people go,' " said Moses nervously. Pharaoh laughed and, to punish his insolence, gave orders that the slaves in the brickfields should make bricks without the straw they needed for the task.

"Let my people go," said Moses, while Aaron worked small wonders, turning a stick into a snake.

"A magic trick," Pharaoh scoffed.

"Let my people go, or the God I serve will do terrible things to make you change your mind."

But Pharaoh only curled his lip in contempt.

Then plagues like the strands of a slave-master's whip fell across Egypt. The Nile turned to blood. Frogs by the millions made fat red blots as they hopped ashore out of the crimson river or rained down out of the sky.

"Let my people go!" said Moses, but Pharaoh would not.

The frogs died in the street and black flies rose off them in swarms.

A plague of flies. God sent diseases that shrank all the fat sleek cows, horses, and camels into bony bags of hide. He plagued smooth Egyptian bodies with lice and boils and rashes. The crops died in the fields.

"Let my people go," said Moses, but Pharaoh would not.

So God browbeat Egypt with fiery hail and freak storms and sent locusts to eat up all the crops.

"Now will you let my people go?" said Moses.

But Pharaoh said, "No."

The last plague was the worst of all. God sent the angel of death — dark as the storm, sharp as the hail, sickening as frogs or boils, winged like a locust, fearsome as a blood-red river. Each Israelite family smeared its doorpost with lamb's blood, and at the sight of that the angel turned away. But under every Egyptian door, shut or open, locked or barred, the angel slipped in like an icy draft and smothered the firstborn of the household.

"Let my people go," said Moses. He had to raise his voice above the noise of weeping mothers, grief-stricken children.

"Go. Get out. Be gone!" said Pharaoh.

Out of Egypt streamed the Israelites, like rivulets joining into brooks, the brooks into a single river. A host of excited, happy faces hurried past the weeping Egyptian mourners, the newly dug graves. There were donkeys and carts, children and old people, women singing and men asking questions: "Where are we going? Where are you taking us, Moses?"

"To a land flowing with milk and honey," he replied, "the one God promised to Abraham." He had no more idea of the way than they had, but he had faith. Suddenly, away in the distance, a whirling spiral of darkness sprang up from the desert sands — a pillar of cloud. "That way," said Moses (who knew a sign when he saw one).

The pillar of cloud led the way by day, a pillar of fire after dark.

Left behind in his empty streets, Pharaoh looked out at his unfinished monuments, his empty brickfields . . . and seethed. "Why did I give in to that insolent Hebrew? Why did I let them go? Fetch them back," he told his army. "Fetch them *all* back!"

At the shores of the Red Sea, the war chariots caught up with the runaways. The whirling pillar of cloud placed itself between them, like a mother shielding her child, but the children of Israel had their backs to the sea and nowhere to run.

Now Moses stretched out his shepherd's staff — the one that had turned the Nile to blood — and he struck the shallow surf. Slowly, sucking and shifting, the waves writhed. Like two sleeping people rolling away from one another, the two sides of the sea rolled apart, leaving a path of glistening wet sand, rocks, starfish, and weed.

The fleeing Israelites started along this corridor through the ocean glass-walled with water fifty fathoms high. They carried their children, their lambs, their bundles, held their breath between their teeth.

The watching Egyptians gaped and gasped at the sight of a sea splitting in two. Chariot horses trembled in their traces. Then the pillar of cloud vanished. "After them, men!" Soft sand sucked at the chariot wheels, but in the Egyptians plunged, into the heart of the hollowed sea.

"They're coming after us!" cried the Israelites, looking back over their shoulders, breaking into a run. They ran and they stumbled and they clambered out onto the sunlit stones of the far shore.

Then the walls of water crumbled, and the waves remembered to break. Like curtains being drawn closed, the two sides of the ocean rejoined. The seething foam tumbled with Egyptian wheels, helmets, reins, curses, whips, swords and prayers.

On the far side of the sea, the children of Israel lay panting on the shore. Behind them the smooth and silent sea sighed; ahead of them stretched the empty desert, humming with heat. After generations of slavery, they were finally free!

Free to do what? To go thirsty? To starve? After the happiness, panic quickly set in. The flat, hard bread they had hurriedly baked for the journey was gone now. How far must they travel to reach the land of milk and honey? "Trust God," Moses had said, but for how long?

Next morning they woke, and the ground was caked with cobwebs — or was it thistledown, or moss? Hungry little ones plucked at it and put it to their mouths. Mothers snatched it from them, sniffed the strange stuff, touched it to their tongues.

It was food.

"Eat," said Moses. "It is 'manna.' God has sent it. He has spread the desert like a table for you."

The manna would not keep. It was no good stuffing it in saddlebags or baskets, to eat the next day. By noon it had withered and shriveled away. But each morning there was more. And so the children of Israel gradually learned to trust God's promise, day by day, to feed them, to guide them and to take care of them.

———————

"I've found a sandwich!" exclaimed the boy, looking over into the pew behind him. "Someone's left half a sandwich!" and he reached over for it.

"You can't eat that!"

"Why? Oh, is it yours? Sorry."

"No! It's not mine. But you don't know who left it there or how old it is!" He watched with disgust as the boy bit into the sandwich, but he felt compelled to ask, "What is it?"

The boy shrugged and chewed. "Manna sandwich, maybe."

THE FOREIGNER

The next morning, the boy did not come. Food poisoning, thought the old man. That sandwich. And he was angry, because he could not concentrate on the sheaf of corn he was carving. Fool boy. Even when he was not there, he could manage to make a nuisance of himself.

Then after lunch he came, his hair wet from swimming. "Didn't Jesus have any girl ancestors?" he asked, not wasting time on "Hello."

"Well, of course he did!"

"But they aren't allowed to climb in the Jesse tree, right?"

"Of course they are . . . in fact this sheaf of corn I'm carving right now . . ." The old man broke off as soon as he realized his mistake, but it was too late. He was obliged to tell the story of Ruth.

Ruth was a Moabite, born in Moab, brought up with a Moabite religion. But when she married a foreigner — an Israelite living in her country — she found that she liked the thoughts in his head, the beliefs in his heart. She began to say her prayers to the God of the Israelites. Even when her husband died, Ruth did not fall back into her Moabite ways. Her greatest friend in the world was her mother-in-law, Naomi.

Naturally, Naomi was heartbroken: her son was dead and she was marooned, penniless, in a foreign land. "I must go back home to my own people," she told Ruth. "I can't stay here with nothing to live on."

"I'll come with you," said Ruth.

"But you were born here in Moab! Your people will look after you! You don't want to be burdened with me!"

Gently Ruth took hold of the old woman's hand and laid it against her own cheek. "Wherever you go, I shall go. Your people will be my people and your God my God."

So Ruth and Naomi made the long journey to Bethlehem — two women without a man to keep them fed, sheltered, or safe. They had no land to farm, no flocks to tend. In those days, life for a widow was harder than hard, and Ruth had two mouths to feed, not just one.

It was harvest time in the fields. Ruth went with the other women to glean — to pick up the ears of corn left behind by the reapers as they hacked down the crop. The spiky stubble pricked her ankles and hands; her back ached. The other women shunned her, this foreign woman, this Moabite beauty. For every grain of corn she picked up, Ruth let a tear fall.

That was when Boaz, the owner of the field, saw her. He was a good, kind man. He asked about the foreign beauty weeping amid his corn—and he liked what he heard. A remarkable girl, indeed, to leave home for the sake of her mother-in-law. Boaz called her over. "When you rest," he said, "feel free to sit down with my reapers." And he made sure that the reapers were not unkind to her and that they let plenty of grain fall as they hacked their way through the corn. Ruth told Naomi all about it when she got home that evening. And Naomi began to think what could be done.

Naomi may have had no money to share with her daughter-in-law, but she did have the wisdom of age. "I am distantly related to Boaz. He's a good man . . . Ruth, I want you to do exactly as I tell you . . ." And of course Ruth did, though the advice was astounding . . . and more than a little frightening.

Later, Boaz went to work on the threshing floor, pounding the ears of corn with a leather flail until they jumped like crickets. The air around him was soon smoky with dust. Threshing is exhausting work, and no sooner had Boaz eaten his supper than he curled up alongside the threshing floor and rested his head on a bale of straw. His graying hair was grayer still with corn dust, his mind busy with business and prayers. He dozed.

When he stirred, the midnight threshing floor was pitch black but for the merest moonlight. To his dismay, Boaz felt a warm weight resting across his ankles — "Who's there?" — and sat bolt upright, only to find the Moabite girl lying across his feet. Boaz blushed, and so did Ruth, though the dark hid their blushes. Her breath shook with fear, but she spoke the words Naomi had told her.

"I am Ruth, your servant. You are a kinsman of mine. Let me creep under your cloak and be safe."

Boaz did better. He married Ruth and gave her and her mother-in-law a comfortable home and a place where they belonged. There were whispers among the gossips, of course. Boaz betrothed? Boaz married? And to a foreigner? But God himself had whispered in Boaz's ear. God, who had once made Eve as a helpmate for Adam, had brought to Bethlehem a wife of such courage and devotion, of such beauty and selflessness, that she would make his town immeasurably richer. The gossip soon faded. On the day Ruth gave birth to Boaz's son, they brought flowers and little presents and broad sunny smiles.

———————————

"What was the baby called?"

The carpenter pinched the bridge of his nose with finger and thumb. "You make me weary with your everlasting questions. Let me see now. Obed. The child's name was Obed."

"And what are you going to carve for him?"

The carpenter waved his chisel irritably. "Obed's not important. He just grew up to be the father of Jesse and the grandfather of —"

"At last! Jesse!" exclaimed the boy loudly, and set the church ringing. "Jesse of the Jesse tree!" The boy padded away down the church aisle. His hair was dry now. At the door he turned and called, "Obed was important, I bet! To Ruth and Boaz, I bet!"

"I didn't mean — " said the old man, but the church door banged, and he was alone. He went back to his work, but found himself saying (as if the boy were still there), "I didn't mean he wasn't important. I only meant that Obed doesn't have a story — written down — in the Bible. That's all I meant." And he carved a little O above the sheaf of corn — O for Obed. It was only as big as a grain of corn or a teardrop. No one would know it was there, except him. But it made him feel better, knowing he had not left out Obed altogether.

"Speak, Lord, for Your Servant Is Listening"

"Be careful where you step! I put down my spectacles somewhere and now I can't find them." The carpenter was in a towering rage. His woodworking tools lay scattered at the foot of the Jesse tree: without his glasses he could not see to work. Without his glasses he could not see to find his glasses.

The boy bounded about the church, searching the side chapels and looking under the pews. "You should have a spare pair."

"Do you think I'm made of money?"

"A spare pair of eyes, I meant. What's this you're carving? It looks like Aladdin's lamp." He returned to the Jesse tree and stood rubbing it with a cuff of his sweatshirt.

"It's a jar of oil," growled the carpenter. "In the old days, a man became king only when the high priest anointed his head with holy oil."

"So is this a story about a king or a priest?"

"What story? Was I telling a story?"

"You may as well," said the boy, making himself comfortable. "Until your glasses turn up."

There was once a woman who so longed for a child that she made a deal with God. "Grant me a son, Lord," she prayed, "and I'll give him back to you!" True to her word, when Samuel was born, his mother loved him, nursed him, enjoyed and taught him . . . then gave him up to be a servant in the temple at Shiloh.

Eli, the high priest, was a very old man — older than I am — and blind, pretty near blind. He had sons who would take over from him when he died. But in the meantime, he had Samuel to be his hands and eyes. Priest and boy lived out their days and nights in the temple, sleeping on the floor, in the big darkness. During the day, there was always noise — singing, chanting, the murmur of doves, the twitter of sparrows. At night, the silence was solid black. But it held no terror for either of them. Eli's whole world was dark, and for Samuel there was the glimmer of the sacred lamp burning like a single, watchful eye.

"Samuel! Samuel!"

The boy raised himself up on one elbow. The words had awakened him. The old priest plainly needed him; perhaps he was ill. Jumping up, Samuel ran to Eli's side. "Yes, master? Here I am."

"What's the matter, child?" said Eli, bleary with sleep.

"You called, so I came."

"I did not call. Go back to sleep, child."

Samuel went and lay down again.

"Samuel! Samuel!" It was a gentle voice and very familiar. Samuel jumped up at once and hurried to Eli's side. "Here I am, master."

"I did not call," said the old priest, opening his blind eyes. "You are dreaming a lot tonight."

So Samuel went back to bed. But again the voice called to him, "Samuel! Samuel!"

Samuel felt his way through the darkness to Eli's side. "You did call, master. You did!"

Then Eli understood. "Go back to bed, child, and if the voice calls again say, 'Speak, Lord, for your servant is listening.' "

All his short life, Samuel had been trained to obey without question or quibble. He went back and laid his head down, though his eyes strained open in the darkness and his heart was jumping.

"Samuel! Samuel!" called the voice, patiently awaiting an answer.

Samuel knelt on his bedroll. "Speak, Lord, for your servant is listening!"

And God spoke to him: out of the gentle dark, out of the glow of the sacred lamp, or out of the most distant galaxy. "I have news for Eli — bad news — and you must be the one to break it. His sons are not fit to do the work their father has done. They will not live to take his place. You are my choice, Samuel. You are the one I need."

When the voice fell silent, Samuel did not want to tell the good old man such crushing news. But the next morning, Eli was anxious to know: "What did God say to you, boy? What secrets did he entrust to you?"

Samuel was afraid that his words would kill the old man then and there, but he spoke them faithfully, and Eli nodded, fixing his shineless eyes on the shineless future. Then he patted the air with a trembling hand. "God is good," he said. "Let it come."

The Jesse tree stood incomplete. Its lower branches were crowded with leaves and symbols, but the upper branches were still trapped inside the slab of oak, like something ancient and only part unearthed.

"I see them!" cried the boy, his sharp eyes catching the glint of glass on a stone window ledge. He ran and fetched the spectacles, and the carpenter, after dabbing his eyes, crammed the glasses back onto his face.

"Shoo now!" he growled. "I've wasted enough time today. I have to get back to work."

"I thought it would be Jesse today," called the boy from the porch. "After the O you carved for Obed."

"O? What O? Oh, that O," said the carpenter gruffly. "Today Samuel, tomorrow Jesse." Then he wondered why he had said it. The boy would come back now for sure, expecting another story.

THE SHEPHERD KING

It was not the grief of his sons' deaths that killed Eli. In the temple at Shiloh was kept Israel's most precious treasure: the ark of the covenant. One day . . .

"What, Noah's ark, you mean?" the boy interrupted.

"Oh, child! This happened hundreds, maybe thousands of years after the flood."

No, the Ark of the Covenant was a wooden box with carved angels decorating it. (What a piece of work it must have been!) It was used to hold the Ten Commandments, God's holy laws, and it was the holiest thing in all Israel. The mere sight of it made the Israelites feel invincible! Well, the hostile Philistines knew this, and when the ark was taken into battle, they attacked and captured it, knowing the loss would rip the very heart out of Israel. When Eli heard the news, he died of grief.

Samuel became priest instead of Eli's sons. As he grew older, God would often stoop down to whisper in his ear — news, commands, encouragement. It was time for Israel to have a king, said God, and Samuel was the one to anoint that king.

The man Samuel anointed first was Saul: a great man, a great soldier. Saul was like a pillar of fire leading the Israelites through every hardship, keeping them safe from their enemies.

But power does strange things to people. Saul began to forget that his crown had been given to him by God. He took no notice of Samuel's advice. Things started to go wrong. Seeing their chance, Israel's enemies closed in, like prowling wolves when a campfire goes out.

Samuel was a prophet. Not only could he hear God's voice, but he could see forward through time, as through a dazzle of light. Soon he could foresee a time when Saul would not be king. God even told him where to look for Saul's replacement: among the sons of Jesse. But which of Jesse's many sons should he choose? That was the question.

They were all fine, strong boys, tall and muscular.
They might all make good warriors in the king's
army. As Samuel met first one, then another, then
a third, no lamp flickered in his soul; no voice
spoke to him out of the farthest galaxies,
saying, "This is the one."

"Are these all the sons you have?" he asked
Jesse.

"All but for David, my youngest. He's out
with the sheep," said Jesse.

David was sent for, and Samuel studied
him, like a shepherd examining a newborn
lamb . . . Yes. There it was. The face he had
been waiting to see. He anointed David with
holy oil — just as he might a king. "Say
nothing," he told father and son. "Not now.
Not yet."

Times were bad. The Philistines were winning the
war. David's older brothers went to fight in the king's army,
but David was too young. He was trusted with no more than fetching and carrying.
"Take your brothers these rations, David," said Jesse. "And come straight back."

Long before David reached the camp of King Saul, he could hear the Philistine
army jeering. Even as he handed his brothers the cheese and bread and raisins, he
could hear the sneering jibes coming from across the valley: the laughter and the
catcalls.

"What's going on?" he asked.

"The Philistines have issued a challenge — their champion against ours — and
there's no one to answer it."

"Why? Is he so terrifying?" asked David.

"Have you seen him?" groaned a nearby soldier. "Tall as a horse!"

"Broad as a bull!" said another.

"Twice the size of a normal man! We don't stand a chance . . ."

Inside his tent, King Saul fumed with helpless rage. "Does no one dare fight this
man-mountain? Is Israel full of cowards?"

But it was not a matter of cowardice. If one brave soul was to fight Goliath and lose, then all Israel would be lost. And no one wanted to be responsible for that.

"There's a boy here who says he will fight," said the guard at the tent doorway.

It was David.

At first, Saul turned his back and laughed. But David ducked inside the tent. "Out in the fields, guarding my father's sheep, I've fought off a lion before now — wolves and bears . . . God helped me then. How much worse can this big bully be?"

There must have been something in the boy's face — the same thing Samuel had seen. King Saul believed him. In fact, he began to take off his armor and hang it on David's small frame: leather tunic, chain mail, a big brass helmet. David sagged under the weight, like a tree under snow. His legs bowed. "I can't wear this!" he protested. And he went, as he was, to fight the giant called Goliath.

"WHAT HAVE YOU SENT ME? A STICK TO PICK MY TEETH WITH?" roared Goliath. He cast a shadow as big as a building.

David bent down as he crossed the stream, chose a handful of round pebbles and put them into his shepherd's bag.

"DO THE ISRAELITES THINK I WILL LAUGH MYSELF TO DEATH?" snorted Goliath. The noise of his armor was like a cart rattling over bumpy ground. David placed a stone into the pouch of his sling.

"COME CLOSER, BOY, AND I'LL PULL YOU LIKE A WISHBONE!" boomed Goliath. His massive feet raised clouds of dust, as if he were ablaze.

But David did not need to go any closer. He whirled his sling — it made a high, eerie whooping — then let the pebble fly.

"WELL? ARE YOU GOING TO FIGHT ME OR JUST ST —" The giant broke off, his mouth a black circle of surprise. He reeled, he staggered. His hand went up to his forehead. Then he fell. The ground shuddered.

With a single gasp, the Philistines began to run. They had lost their champion; they had lost their advantage. The Israelites went after them like cats after mice.

King Saul gazed at the shepherd boy David with admiration and joy. "From today I shall keep you by me all the time!" he declared, and hugged the boy close. Sweat from his throat trickled down onto David's hair, just like the oil used to anoint a king.

"King Saul should have known," said the boy, "that David was more of a threat than Goliath."

The carpenter looked at him sharply. "Saul was his own worst enemy. He had a dirty temper and fits of black misery. David could play the harp; sometimes that soothed Saul's dark moods. But sometimes Saul would still throw things and rant and curse like a madman."

The boy gave a lopsided sort of smile and looked firmly at the floor. "Some people are like that," he said. "They can't help it."

DANCING

A car had parked outside the church and its radio was playing very loudly — a thump-thumping rhythm that made the water in the font ripple. The boy jumped about to the music, trying to tap his bare heels together in mid-air.

"Confounded racket," complained the old man. "Stop that jigging, can't you? Remember where you are."

"Is that another rule? No dancing in church?"

The carpenter made a noise like a grumpy camel. "Humph. Do you want me to go on telling you about David or not?"

———————

Luckily, David found a good friend in the king's son, Jonathan. In fact, David and Jonathan became the kind of friends who start singing in the same key, who start speaking at the same moment. They were inseparable. Together, David and Jonathan and King Saul cut down the Philistines like a field of corn. As the conquering army trooped home, women and girls came out to dance and sing in the streets. "Saul has killed thousands! David has killed tens of thousands!"

Over and over, Saul muttered the words under his breath. They rankled. "David . . . tens of thousands." Jealousy chewed on him like a dog. Suddenly the mere sight of David sitting there, plucking a gentle tune on his harp, was enough to cloud Saul's vision with red smoke. Picking up a spear, he hurled it.

David ducked. The spear hit the wall and stuck there, trembling. David fled.

Jonathan went after him. "Stop! Wait! I can talk my father around! I've done it before, haven't I?" The friends clung to each other, dreading the power and spite of the king. "Hide there, behind those rocks," said Jonathan. "Tomorrow I'll come and practice archery here.

If I shoot short, it means it's safe for you to come back. If I shoot past you . . ."

It was hard to think about — best friends might need to be parted.

The next day Jonathan went out with his bow. His fingers fumbled the bowstring. His arrows flew, with a noise like sucking breath, way out over the rocks, over the crouching figure of David.

David had to leave. It was no longer safe to stay. Madness, like a raven, sat on the king's shoulder, whispering terrible thoughts into his ear. Saul now looked on David as an enemy to be hunted down and killed.

David could have fought back, he was a good enough soldier. Once he even chanced on Saul in a cave and could have killed him then and there. But David settled for slicing the fringe off Saul's cloak. "If I wanted to kill you, I could have done so today," he said, half reproachful, half taunting, "but I would never lift a finger against you."

Saul's heart was no more softened than a stone in a stream. He went to war with David, body and soul.

Faced with this madness, some of Saul's troops deserted him and went over to David's side. The Philistines, meanwhile, rubbed their hands with glee and closed in for the kill. In a disastrous battle, Saul and three of his sons were killed. One of those sons was Jonathan.

"Oh, Jonathan! Jonathan!" The cry that broke from David's throat was like a bell falling from its tower and breaking. Thanks to the Philistines, David had become king of Israel . . . and he was inconsolable.

But King David believed in God and he believed in Israel. He pulled together that unhappy, divided nation, and he rode out to conquer her enemies. When the fighting was over, David determined to take the ark of the covenant (abandoned by the superstitious Philistines) to God's holy city, Jerusalem!

It had been carried into battle, stored in tents and private houses, traipsed through deserts and over mountains . . . Now David brought it on a brand new cart, escorted by a handpicked guard of thirty thousand men. And there were cymbals clashing, tambourines rattling, pipes and lyres and bells, and he danced and he danced . . .

———————

With the music pounding on the car radio outside, the boy, too, began to dance, eyes shut, both hands raised, swaying in time to the beat.

With a clatter, the church door opened and a lady with her arms full of gladioli came in. At the sight of a barefoot boy dancing up and down the aisle, her mouth and eyes narrowed to slits. "What is that child doing, Mr. Butterfield?"

The carpenter's mild reply shocked her even more: "Just dancing, Mrs. Grimley. Like King David did in Jerusalem. Dancing before the Lord."

THE WISDOM OF SOLOMON

Near the jar of oil that stood for Samuel, Mr. Butterfield had carved a sling and a crown to represent King David. Close by, he carved a gateway: two pillars and an arched entry over the top.

"Is that David's palace?" asked the boy. The carpenter had grown so used to these daily visits that he no longer jumped when a shadow fell across his work and a small finger reached out to stroke the wood.

"It is the great temple in Jerusalem. Solomon's temple. You must have heard of Solomon. There were fairy tales written about him, he was so famous. Flying carpets, genies in bottles, that sort of nonsense."

"Can't you do genies, then?" said the boy, as if gates were boring by comparison.

"I'm not carving fairy stories; I'm carving Bible stories . . . At least I would be if people would just let me get on. Solomon's temple was real." And before anyone asked him to, he was telling the story of Solomon's temple.

Solomon was David's son, but whereas David could be stupid sometimes — downright wicked on occasions — Solomon was as wise and good as any hero in a fairy tale. One day, God asked him what gift he would like best. Now you or I might have said money, or peace and quiet, or long life, but not Solomon. He thought to himself, I'm a king and what do I know about anything? I'm as foolish as a little child. So he asked God to grant him wisdom. God was so delighted that he gave everything else to Solomon as well: good looks, victory, love, wealth — everything.

Out of that wealth, Solomon built a temple. God designed it, and Solomon followed the plans. Together they came up with a building so immense and beautiful that in time the world came to marvel at it. And if visitors were impressed by the temple, they were impressed still more by the king. Solomon was a poet, a statesman, and a judge from the start. It seemed as if there was no problem he could not solve.

So it was to Solomon that people brought their quarrels and lawsuits, their problems and complaints. It was to Solomon that, one day, the two women had come, thrusting the bawling baby into his face, demanding a judgment.

"She is trying to steal my baby! Tell her! Tell her she can't!"

"Don't believe a word she says! He's mine! Anyone will tell you!"

Two women. One child. Someone had to be lying. Rachel said that Miriam had stolen her baby when her own died in the night. Miriam said that it was quite the other way around. The room filled up with the feeble wailing of the baby, the swearing of oaths and the vowing of vows. Solomon put his hands over his ears. "Stop! Silence! Be still!"

All but the baby fell silent. Solomon studied the red-faced creature in his lap. Then he stood up and laid the baby on the floor. Perhaps he did not want his robes dirtied.

"Are there witnesses?" he asked. There were none.

"Is there any proof or evidence?" There was only the word of the women.

"Then let the prize be shared between them!" And he called for a sword. His face was blank, his voice as sharp and cold as a blade.

The women gaped. The king sized up the sword stroke needed — the upswing, the force, the size of the target . . .

Then he lifted the blade to cut the baby in two.

"STOP!" Rachel dropped to her knees and leaned across the baby to shield it with her body. "Stop! Don't! She can have him! I withdraw my claim! Only don't hurt my . . . Don't hurt him! Let him live!" Her eyes were like two deep wounds in her face. Miriam gave a yelp of victory.

Solomon laid aside the sword. "Now I have the evidence I needed," he said, and his voice was soft as velvet, as gentle as a woman's. Tenderly lifting the baby, he laid it, not in Miriam's reaching arms, but in Rachel's. "A child's true mother would sooner break her own heart than harm her child," said Solomon. "I know now that he is yours."

The court ushers grabbed roughly at Miriam — the proven liar, the wicked stealer of the baby — threatening her with fines, punishment, imprisonment. But Solomon waved them away. "Last night, this woman's child died. Has she not lost enough already?"

The court session was over. The palace fell silent, but for the distant bang and clatter of building work up at the great temple. Solomon's soul turned inward, to that quiet inner reservoir of stillness that made him so wise. This was where he talked to God and composed poetry about love.

Strangely enough, at the heart of Solomon's temple, there was just such a place. People called it the Holy of Holies — an inner room furnished with stillness, where holiness itself could be found.

For a long time, neither of them spoke. Then the boy said, "Solomon couldn't have been all that foolish to begin with, or he would never have asked God for wisdom, would he?"

"True."

"Did he know about you and me, old Solomon?"

Mr. Butterfield narrowed his eyes. "No-o-o," he admitted cautiously. "He wasn't a prophet."

"But we know about him, right?"

"Hmm," said Mr. Butterfield, scenting a trick question.

". . . So that makes us wiser than Solomon, doesn't it?!" And the boy ran out of the church, laughing delightedly.

Hearing the door reopen, Mr. Butterfield retaliated, "You're not wise, lad! You're just too clever for your own boots!" Then he glanced up, grinning . . . and saw that he had insulted the minister by mistake.

THE IDOL AND
THE STILL SMALL VOICE

"So why wasn't Jesus a king," asked the boy the next day, "if his ancestors were David and Solomon?"

The old man examined the blade of his chisel. "Solomon's kingdom didn't last. After he died, it was carved in two by rival kings. Some time later, Ahab came to power in one of these territories. King Ahab was as wicked as Solomon was good.

In fact, there was only one person in the whole world more wicked than Ahab, and Ahab married her — a woman called Jezebel."

When Jezebel married Ahab, she brought her religion with her. She wasn't like Ruth. She didn't learn to love the religion of the Hebrews, the Israelites. No, Queen Jezebel chose to hate it. She set out to destroy the Israelite God and replace him with her own—the false god Baal. So the first thing she did was to order the death of every Israelite prophet: no mercy. No pity. No survivors.

Except Elijah, who escaped the terrible slaughter. With God's help, he found himself a hiding place, like a water rat, on the bank of the River Jordan.

No food. No friends. Nowhere to turn.

Elijah curled up and closed his eyes, barely wanting to open them ever again. When he looked through his lashes, he saw black birds above him. Crows circling over a carcass, he thought.

But they were not crows. They were ravens, and in their beaks they carried bread and meat. Like small jet-black angels, they waited on Elijah. Week after week, they fed him, preserving his life. The question was: for what?

The Israelites wept. The clouds above them ought to have wept, too, at the death of so many holy prophets, but they shed not one drop. In fact, they melted away like manna at noon, and left only a brass-colored sun that baked the country dry.

No water. No crops. Famine.

"Go to the city of Zarephath," said God to Elijah, "and do as I tell you . . ."

At the city gates, Elijah met a woman, thin as a stalk of corn. "Give me some water and something to eat," the prophet said.

"Me, sir?" she replied. "I'm here gathering wood to cook one last mouthful of bread. Tonight all our food will be gone, and we shall sit down together and starve, my boy and I."

But Elijah simply asked again, "Give me something to eat."

Out of charity or out of despair, the widow agreed, knowing this guest of hers would empty her flour bin and her bottle of oil once and for all.

But no! After supper, she found they were both still half full! In fact, days came and days went, and still the bin and the bottle were not emptied. "You have been good to one of God's prophets," Elijah explained, smiling at the joy a simple miracle could give.

Within weeks that joy was gone. "Is this how your great God rewards me?"

The widow stood in the doorway, her little boy in her arms. The child was dead.

Elijah could find nothing to say to comfort her. He spoke to God instead. "Are you really going to let this happen to a woman who befriended me?" he implored, taking the little body in his arms, stumbling up the steps of the house. Up in his room, he laid the boy down. Three times he flung himself across the little body, berating God, pleading with God.

With a noise like a fire sucking in air, the boy began to cough, his eyes to flicker, his chest to heave. Behind Elijah, the widow laughed and wept and wept and laughed, spreading her palms to the sky. "A man of God! A man of God! Now I know you are a man of God!"

When God put life back into that little boy, he put it back, too, into Elijah. Suddenly the prophet was filled with the certainty that he could do anything.

He was simply a tool in the hand of God (and God is a craftsman, after all).

Elijah went to King Ahab. "Abandon your idol worship! Turn back to the one true God!" he demanded. "Summon the people to Mount Carmel, and I'll show you the difference between a false god and the real thing!"

Two altars stood on the mountainside, one built by the queen's prophets of Baal,

the other by Elijah. There was no difference between them, though —
stones, sticks, a sacrificial ox — and neither was lit. The pagan
prophets began to dance and to chant, to sway and jump and roll
their eyes. "Send down fire, O mighty Baal!" they wailed. "Devour
this, our sacrifice!"

"What's the matter?" asked Elijah, after this had gone on for a
while. "Maybe Baal's asleep! Call louder!"

So the queen's prophets lunged and pranced, yelped and
whooped. "SEND DOWN FIRE, O BAAAAAL!"

No spark. No flicker. No answer.

Then Elijah raised his eyes to the sky and simply asked once
for the gift of fire.

It was as if the sun had lobbed a fireball. It was as if the
stones themselves had burst into flame. With a smell of roast
meat, a welter of orange fire swallowed up Elijah's sacrifice.
The sea of faces watching from the valley below turned
orange in the glow, then disappeared as the crowd fell
flat and cried, in one voice, "The Lord is God!"

Elijah, his face red from the heat of the fire,
looked over at King Ahab. "Go home," he said.
"The drought is over."

From the cloudless blue of the sky, this seemed
as unlikely as . . . as, well, fire falling from
heaven, but Ahab had learned better than
to scoff at Elijah. Sure enough, as he
drove his chariot back to his palace,
the sky filled up with billowing
rain clouds, and sharp drops of
rain began to pierce the dust.

"Where are my prophets?"
Jezebel demanded when Ahab
returned home.

"They failed," said King Ahab.
"The true God sent fire; theirs

didn't. Everyone saw."

Queen Jezebel, however, did not fall on her face and worship God. " 'Where are my prophets?' I asked."

"Elijah killed them after his God sent fire."

Jezebel's face froze over like a pond. She called for a servant and sent this message to Elijah: "May I die, too, unless I kill you within the day."

Elijah's newfound bravery melted away. He fled for his life — out of the royal city of Jezreel, out of the wet, greening countryside, out into the desert.

No food. No water. No courage.

How had anything changed for him? He was back where he had started, and so tired that he almost wished the miraculous fire had swallowed him, too, off the face of the earth.

He woke to the sound of a voice in his ear, a sweet smell of baking, a hand on his sleeve. "Eat, Elijah. Drink. Then go to Mount Horeb. God is waiting." By the time he had shaken off sleep, there was no one to be seen, but a container of water and a slab of cake stood beside his head.

For forty days and forty nights, that jug and cake kept him going, as he trekked across the lonely desert towards the holy mountain of Horeb. Once there, Elijah stood on the mountaintop and listened for the voice of God.

Lately, he had grown better at listening.

A blustering, bullying, bellowing wind came and buffeted the mountain, uprooting bushes, wildly wailing and whipping up the dirt . . . But the wind was not God speaking.

An earthquake took hold of the roots of the mountain and shook it until boulders bounced by and stones skittered downhill in landslides . . . But the earthquake was not God speaking.

A firestorm besieged the mountain, licking up every leaf and twig, scouring Horeb bare. Elijah was wound in a shroud of black and choking smoke . . . But the fire was not God speaking.

Last of all, in the silence that followed the wind and the earthquake and the fire, a calm, small voice spoke to Elijah. Elijah knew that this was the voice of God.

"Find the men called Hazael and Jehu and anoint them kings over Israel. Find the young man Elisha and teach him all you know; he must take your place when you are gone."

Elijah bowed his head. He knew he would obey. He knew that God saw far into the future — farther than any prophet — beyond wise kings and evil ones, beyond good times and bad. Elijah would go where he was sent and speak the words God put into his mouth. He was a tool, after all, in the hands of a craftsman.

"Was it angel cake, do you think?" said the boy abruptly.

"Was what angel cake?" asked Mr. Butterfield, confused for a moment.

"The cake that the angels delivered to Elijah in the desert. I like angel cake."

"I think it's unlikely."

"I expect those ravens were making up for the time when they didn't find any dry land for Noah!"

'They would have been very old ravens in that case," said the carpenter, carving the delicate feathering into a raven's wing.

"Descendants, then. Ravens from the same family tree."

"Oh, certainly," said Mr. Butterfield, nodding earnestly. "Have to be, wouldn't they? Anyway, where else would you find a family of ravens, if it wasn't in a family tree? Tee-hee."

It was the closest he had come to making a joke for several years. Mr. Butterfield began to whistle a breathy tune.

WAR AND PEACE

"Was Elijah one of Jesus' ancestors?"

Mr. Butterfield folded his bottom lip over the top one. It was far too difficult to explain.

"Well, what about Elisha, then? Was he?"

"No, no, no. He and Elijah were prophets. Can't you see? They have a separate bough to themselves. But they often appear on Jesse trees. It's traditional."

"Why? Why are they there? If they weren't ancestors of Jesus?"

The carpenter dropped the little scraping tool he was using to hollow out the raven's eye. "It's traditional, I told you. Tradition . . ."

"But you must know," insisted the boy.

"Of course I know. Of course I do!" Mr. Butterfield mopped his forehead with a dirty rag. "The prophets are there because . . . because they knew Jesus was coming. Even hundreds of years before he came, they caught glimpses of him in their dreams! They pictured him in their visions. They promised God's people that he really was coming — a redeemer, a rescuer, someone who would forgive them all their mistakes. 'A descendant of Jesse will appear . . .' — that's what the prophet Isaiah told them. 'A shoot will spring from the stock of Jesse and from his roots a bud will blossom.' Long before the prophets, Joseph, Moses and all the people I've told you about trusted God to rescue them. But the prophets knew something Joseph and Moses didn't. God had told them he would send a Savior. The Messiah."

"Someone to fight off their worst giants!"

"Someone to guide them back to Paradise Garden."

"So where are the prophets? Show me!"

Mr. Butterfield pointed out a row of symbols dangling from one bough of his oaken Jesse tree. "Here, look. Here's one of the ravens that fed Elijah in the desert. Here's Nehemiah's trowel . . . (He encouraged the Israelites to rebuild the walls of Jerusalem after they were destroyed.) And here's a plough for Isaiah."

"Was he a farmer, then?"

"I told you. Weren't you listening? He was a prophet."

"I thought prophesying might be a part-time job. Why a plough?"

"Because he said there would come a time, one day, when there would be no more war, and people would hammer their swords into blades for their ploughs. Imagine. Peace. Blessed peace." Mr. Butterfield said it wistfully, wishfully. His head was spinning. "Next, I'll carve a bear here, to represent Elisha . . ."

"Ooh, a bear! Why a bear? Tell about the bear!"

The questions buzzed like hornets around Mr. Butterfield's head. "Because a crowd of good-for-nothing small boys waylaid him and jeered at him and called him names and chanted, 'Go on, Baldy! Go on, Baldy!' and mocked him and pestered him until he couldn't stand any more, so he cursed them black and blue, and two she-bears came rampaging out of a wood and ate them all up! NOW WILL YOU LET ME GET BACK TO WORK?!"

The boy bolted.

A moment later, the carpenter started after him, swaying unsteadily from foot to foot, arms upraised and looking very like a charging bear. "Stop! Wait!"

Clang! The big metal latch of the door clacked shut.

He banged up against the baptismal font, making the water slop. Then he steadied himself and opened the latch, but the street outside was already empty. Wearily he slumped down on a big oak chest by the door.

"I'll bet Elisha regretted that temper of his," he said under his breath. "I know I do."

The bear that he carved that day was not very fierce at all. In fact it wore an anxious sort of a smile and stood on its hind legs, stretching its neck for all the world as if watching out for a long-awaited friend.

Dumbstruck!

Mr. Butterfield waited. He did not know what he was waiting for exactly, but he waited. Just when he finally had the chance to work undisturbed, he could not seem to get going. He had nearly reached the crown of the Jesse tree — the boughs in which he would carve the family of Jesus himself . . . And yet, Mr. Butterfield waited, and the longer he waited, the more restless he grew. His big shoes crunched the dust up and down the aisle, and even took him up to the altar to gaze at the figures in the stained-glass windows. As the light faded behind the windows, the saints and apostles melted away. But Mr. Butterfield sat down where he was, in the soft gloom, waiting.

"Are you allowed up there?" It was the boy.

"So long as I show respect," said Mr. Butterfield. The bones of his knees clicked as he stood up. "Once upon a time, only the priest came past the altar rail. People aren't so strict nowadays." He waited for the boy to ask for a story. "I mean, in the temple in Jerusalem, only certain priests could go into the Holy of Holies, the sacred center. It was hidden out of sight by a curtain.

"Jesus' uncle Zechariah wasn't allowed in there, even though he worked in the temple. Zechariah loved his work, loved his wife Elizabeth, and loved living in Jerusalem. He was a man at peace — except that he had no children, and more than anything, Zechariah wanted a son." Mr. Butterfield broke off.

"He was like you, you mean," said the boy. "Go on."

Zechariah loved the temple: its soft gloom, its starry candle flames, its heady scent of incense, the quiet babble of voices discussing the Scriptures. There were things in there so precious and so ancient that they filled him with wonder. But when Zechariah first saw the figure standing beside the altar of incense, he was taken aback.

"Greetings, Zechariah," said the stranger with the candlelit face. "Congratulations. You are about to become a father."

Zechariah almost laughed, almost wept. All his life, he and Elizabeth had longed for a child. Now it was far too late. "Don't make fun of me. I'm old! How could . . . ?"

But the figure cloaked in sweet-smelling smoke held up a hand. "You must call him John. He will herald the coming of the Messiah, the Savior. He will be a voice shouting in the wilderness!"

At that, Zechariah put a hand to his throat, another to his heart, his aching, thundering heart . . .

The handful of people praying in the temple looked up as Zechariah stumbled forward. His eyes were full of candlelight. His hands fluttered like doves. His mouth opening as if to speak . . . but no words came out. Zechariah had been struck dumb.

Even when his wife, Elizabeth, half amazed, half terrified, whispered to her husband that she was expecting a child, Zechariah could only grin and nod and scratch his joy on a wax tablet using a stylus. His writing looked like angels flying across the white wax.

"So who was the stranger?" asked the boy.

"Well, bless me, an angel, of course! The angel Gabriel, at a guess. God's special messanger: that's how I like to think of Gabriel. I picture him, breaking the news to Zechariah, then strolling down the road to Nazareth — taking weeks about it, but whistling all the way — to speak to Mary!"

"So why didn't the angel just tell everyone? He could have saved himself lots of tramping about. Why didn't angel Gabriel just roll back the sky and shout, 'HE'S COMING! THE RESCUER! YOUR SUPERHERO!' "

Mr. Butterfield scratched his chin with his chisel thoughtfully. "Maybe it's not everyone who can see angels. Maybe it's only certain people."

"You could be right," said the boy with an odd smile, which he seemed to brush off with one hand and slip into his shirt pocket along with the sawdust.

MARY

"I can see it all in my head," said Mr. Butterfield suddenly. "I have to work while I can picture it." As he worked, Mr. Butterfield went on with the story, even though no one had asked him to.

———————

Mary was a good girl. Everyone said so. In fact, people probably never spoke about her at all, because gossips are only interested in people's faults and mistakes, and Mary did nothing wrong. She was promised in marriage to the local carpenter, Joseph. The idea pleased her, because it pleased everyone else, and happiness made Mary happy.

It was a warm day, a low sun. The olive trees wore capes of light. The herbs between her fingers gave off a dizzying fragrance. The figure in white, striding along the roadway, reflected the sun so brightly as to dazzle Mary.

"Greetings, Mary," he said. "Don't be afraid. God holds you in his mind and in his heart. I have news for you."

Mary did not jump up or run into the house. She simply greeted the stranger.

"The Lord God has chosen you, Mary, to give birth to a son. You must call him Jesus."

Mary did not faint or laugh, though her face grew paler. "How can that be? I'm not even married!"

"Mary, you're the most blessed woman alive. God's Spirit will overshadow you. He will entrust you with his own Son," said the angel. "If you are willing."

Mary did not protest or cry. She did not speak of the shame her family would feel, the things Joseph would say. She simply lowered her head. "Let it be as God wishes," was all she said.

Then the angel was gone, and so was Mary's good name.

———————

"What's wrong with the name Mary?" asked the boy. "It's a perfectly good name."

"Her reputation, I mean," said Mr. Butterfield. "Mary's reputation was gone.

After all, who's going to marry a girl who is already expecting someone else's baby? And who's going to believe a girl who says she's been talking to an angel?"

"Joseph must've," suggested the boy.

"Must he indeed? Must he?" said Mr. Butterfield with an I-know-better sort of look. "If you think that, you're quite mistaken."

Expecting a child?

Joseph was appalled. That spotless, devout, modest young girl everyone spoke so well of was expecting a child? The girl he was supposed to marry? Well, not any more. Joseph's chisel dug into the wood he was carving as if he were cutting Mary out of his heart. No marriage for him.

"A wife like that you can do without!" said his mother that evening, wagging her head, wagging her hands.

Then Joseph dreamed a dream. It cut into his sleep like the teeth of a saw, it was so real. It burned through his closed eyelids and blinded him, it was so bright.

"Don't be afraid to marry Mary," said the angel in his dream. "She has done nothing wrong. The child inside her was placed there by God. He trusts her; so should you. Marry Mary."

The dream trickled out of Joseph's head like sawdust from a lathe. But the joy and the fear remained. Joseph lay on his bed staring at the ceiling. He would marry Mary: a woman more perfect than even he had realized. But now, of course, she would never be entirely his for, first and foremost, she and the child inside her belonged to God.

And what a responsibility! To raise and clothe and feed and educate the Son of God? A tall order for a simple village carpenter. Joseph was late opening his workshop that morning.

"So he was a carpenter, just like you!" said the boy.

"Oh no, lad," said Mr. Butterfield with a sad little smile. "Nothing like me. For one thing, he had a son to look after, didn't he?"

JUMPING FOR JOY

The boy pinched up some sawdust from the floor and trickled it into his shirt pocket.

"Your mother won't thank you for that when she does the laundry," said Mr. Butterfield.

"She won't mind. She'll think it's sand. She says it's like the souvenir from our vacation, the sand in the suitcase. If you met an angel, Mr. Butterfield, would you be happy or scared?"

"A bit of both, I suppose. A bit of each. Like Mary." And on he went with his story.

Mary went to visit her cousin Elizabeth — two women, each expecting a baby, each with an extraordinary story to tell. Anyway, pregnant women always have things to talk about: names and worries, clothes and hopes, feeding and fears, sickness, birth and happiness . . . But even before they met — even as Elizabeth walked up the path to Mary's door — their children were already in touch.

The first Elizabeth knew of her cousin's visit was a riot of joy inside her. Her baby seemed to be leaping and kicking, like King David when he danced before the Lord! Elizabeth hurried outside into the garden, puzzled but laughing and clutching her sides. And there stood her cousin Mary, smiling.

"He knows! My baby knows! He sensed it!" Elizabeth gasped. "Mary! Mary! Blessings on you! The blessings of every mother in the world are on you now and on your unborn baby! Feel! Feel! As you came near, the baby inside me turned somersaults for pure joy!"

Mary laid her hands on her cousin's stomach. (Her own baby's movements were still too tiny to be felt.) It was like a magnet turning towards north. It was like a weathercock turning in the wind. It was like the oceans being tugged to and fro by the moon. The child in Elizabeth's womb, sensing the closeness of Mary's baby, turned in his watery world and reached out a hand. This other child was why he would struggle into the light of day. Here was his reason to live.

"Oh, Mary!" cried Elizabeth. "My baby is jumping for joy!"

———————

"That's John," said the boy. "The baby's who's leaping for joy? That's the baby who has to be called John, right? Angel's orders."

"Angel's orders," Mr. Butterfield agreed. "But nobody knows that yet. Remember: old Zechariah hasn't been able to speak a word ever since that shock in the temple. . ."

"Scary," said the boy, and waited.

"People fret about you when you get older," said Mr. Butterfield a few minutes later. "I dare say they fretted about Zechariah."

"Because he wouldn't speak?"

"Yes, and because he was behaving oddly, too, I suppose. I'm only guessing, mind."

"It would make you behave oddly," the boy agreed. "A thing like that."

———————

Zechariah's family fretted about him, for he was old and frail. For nine months now, he had been unable to speak. They just prayed God would spare him long enough to see his son born.

But Zechariah was not sick. He had lost the power of speech, it is true, but illness had not taken it from him. God had silenced him — but he had given him something far more wonderful in return: a son.

The time came for the child to be named. The neighbors expected him to bear his father's name, but Zechariah wrote wildly on the air.

"Look!" said the neighbors. "He wants to say something! Fetch the wax tablet and the stylus."

Then Zechariah wrote, "His name is John."

Like the Red Sea splashing back onto its dry seabed, words spilled back into Zechariah's throat. "His name is John," he said, again and again. "His name is John. His name is John! His name is John!!" Then he ran to the window and bellowed it into the street, so that a whole flock of doves flew up from the roof opposite: "HIS NAME IS JOHN!"

———————————

The church rang with noise. A starling fluttered about in the organ loft. Mr. Butterfield's chisel began to peck away at the Jesse tree like a spring woodpecker. Suddenly he could picture exactly in his mind how the bough should look . . .

"That's my name," said the boy. "John."

"Is that a fact?" said the old man, but he was paying such attention to his work that it was hard to say if he had heard or not. Tongues of wood curled from under the tip of his chisel, as if they were shaping themselves into words. He worked on, rounding foreheads, creasing robes into pleats and folds. He worked like a man inspired. He did not notice when the boy slipped away, seeing as he did only the grain of the wood and the wood shavings falling to the ground like the molted feathers of angels.

THE WORST OF
ALL POSSIBLE TIMES

"Seems funny," said the boy, appearing as if from nowhere. "You doing Christmas at this time of year."

Outside the church, the sun was fiercely bright. The stained-glass windows blazed blue and red and yellow, as colorful as beach huts. Fairground music floated in at the open door. "That is the next story, isn't it? Christmas?"

"It is," said the carpenter. "Daresay you don't need me to tell you any more. Everyone knows the Christmas story."

"Tell it anyway," said John, and Mr. Butterfield did not put up much of a fight.

The road was rough, the light was failing. More than once, the donkey stumbled over a rut in the ground. "God will take care of everything," said Mary, but Joseph was not so sure. The journey could not have come at a worse time. Mary's baby might be born at any time; she ought to be resting at home, not clinging to the lurching back of a donkey mile after tiring mile.

But the Romans (who had recently made Israel part of their empire) wanted to count the exact number of people in their newly conquered territory. So they had ordered everyone to travel to their hometown and register their names. For Joseph and Mary, that meant traveling to Bethlehem, a small town not far from Jerusalem.

The donkey pitched and rolled. As the roofs of Bethlehem came into sight, the unborn baby flexed his muscles. "It's almost time," said Mary, biting her lip.

A bed. A bed. Joseph must find somewhere for his wife to rest! But the crowds pushed past like a river breaking around an island. The town was full to bursting! Inside the clattering inn, Joseph had to shout to make himself heard. "A bed? Do you have a bed for my wife?"

"You are joking, aren't you?" said the innkeeper. "Not so much as a shelf! The whole tribe of David is in Bethlehem tonight."

Joseph's panic rose. If God really was taking care of everything, he did not seem to be doing a very good job of it. "But her child! The baby! It's coming!"

The innkeeper glanced outside at the woman crouched on the ground beside her donkey. "There's always the stable, I suppose . . . It's not much, but it's shelter. May God be good to you both, my friend. Your baby picked a bad time to be born."

Across the yard the noise from the inn died down; its lamps went out. The only light in the stable came from a wick floating in a bowl of oil. Its flame danced in the eyes of the animals as they watched Joseph rake together a bed of straw. Their ears tilted; the flies settled on their nostrils, but they went on watching, motionless. For the woman was giving birth, and all animals understand the wonder of that.

————————

"No snow, then," said the boy. "There's always snow in the pictures."

"Probably more flies than snow in that part of the world. Flies on the cattle, flies on the donkeys, flies on the dirty straw. People mostly paint it all cozy-looking, with a row of cuddly animals. But that was the whole point, wasn't it? That the Son of God would be born in an ordinary down-to-earth place. That the Maker of the universe would squeeze himself into one, tiny, frail, ordinary, flesh-and-blood human being!

"Must've been a happy time, though. I picture the stars pulsing overhead, and the planets spinning like wheels, and the moon grinning, while the constellations did somersaults across the dark sky!"

The old man and the boy looked at one another. Both of them smiled.

"Flies have thousands of lenses in their eyes," said the boy. "They see everything thousands of times over. If there were all those flies . . . imagine what the flies saw, Mr. Butterfield. Imagine!"

WONDERFUL NEWS

"So there was a sheep in the stable, too, was there?" said the boy. "You've carved a sheep."

Mr. Butterfield held a finger against the side of his nose and winked. "Ah! You don't put sheep in a stable. This sheep was outside," he said.

———————

Just up the way — outside town, beyond a fold or two of hills — some shepherds were sitting on a hillside, all huddled up in their cloaks against the midnight cold. They nodded and dozed.

Then all of a sudden, a light fell through the sky: a shooting star — that's what they thought. But the light grew bigger, formed itself into a shape, hurtled down on them, closer and closer. An eagle after the sheep! one thought and fumbled for his slingshot.

Then the light washed over them, and the sheep glowed snowy white in the brightness, and the shepherds folded their arms over their heads and fell on their faces.

"Don't be afraid," called the figure hanging in mid-air on outstretched wings. "Wonderful news! Wonderful! The Savior of the world is born!" The shepherds lifted first one eyelid, then two. The sheep were gazing upwards, too, yellow eyes changed to gold. "Over there! In Bethlehem! Lying in a cattle manger!" cried the angel. "Go and see for yourselves!" Within a single beat of his outspread wings, the angel was no longer alone. Others, as numberless as starlings at dusk, were there with him, hovering, silvery and singing, high over the sheepy hill: "GLORY TO GOD! PEACE TO HIS PEOPLE ON EARTH!" The singing was as loud as cheering, and there was a kind of music, too, as if someone was using the moon for a gong and was jangling all the stars.

Higher and higher the angel flock flew, shrinking to the size and brightness of fireflies. Darkness washed back again over the landscape in a flood. The sheep shuddered.

But the shepherds were already leaping and loping downhill, stumbling into rabbit holes, laughing and shouting out to one another, "Let's go and see!"

"Wait till I tell my wife!"

"Wait till I tell my children!"

_____

Mr. Butterfield rested his hand on his carving of the manger. "They say the animals spoke on the night Jesus was born. But if they did, they spoke very softly. There was the baby to think of, after all . . ."

_____

Joseph had stuffed clean straw into the animals' feed box, and laid the newborn child in that, for a makeshift cradle. Mary was exhausted, but she didn't get much sleep that night. The baby had just been laid in the manger when the shepherds arrived. Sandals slapping in the yard, eyes still full of light, they bundled inside, noisy with excitement — then suddenly clapped their hands over their mouths, dumbstruck.

They hadn't realized it would be like this: a mucky stable, an ordinary family caught in a crisis — people just like them. The baby looked as small and as feeble as any newborn lamb. And yet for this, those angelic hosts, those creatures of light, those heavenly messengers had sung and danced across the sky, dazzling the dark!

Shyly the shepherds explained themselves, twisting their fingers into nervous knots, apologizing. Then they knelt down, before their trembling knees could give way. And their eyes and minds drank in the wonder of it — that they had been fetched by angels to see this newborn baby king.

———————

"You tell it as if you were there," said the boy.

"While I'm carving this shepherd and his sheep, I *am* there. That's why it's such a treat and a blessing, my line of work."

"But your shepherd wasn't a relation. Jesus wasn't related to any shepherd — unless you count King David."

"Ah! but this shepherd of mine, he's not *just* the Christmas shepherd."

"He isn't?"

"No! When Jesus had grown into a man, he called himself the 'Good Shepherd.' He told a story about a shepherd with a big flock — a hundred sheep. Seems this shepherd loved his sheep so much that when just one went missing, he went out and searched and searched until he found it and brought it safe home. 'I am that good shepherd.' That's what Jesus said. He was trying to explain how he'd come to look after people — to rescue those who were lost. And whenever he explained anything, he used a story."

"So Jesus told stories, too."

Mr. Butterfield was deep in thought. "Huh? Ooh, yes. He was forever telling stories! Stories about sheep, stories about parties; stories about money and friends; finding things, losing things . . . I suppose he grew up listening to the same stories I've been telling you, and it made a storyteller out of him. Besides . . . how could I leave out the shepherds? They were witnesses! They were there! They saw what happened!"

"So," said the boy. "Make me see."

THE CUNNING AND THE WISE

"Look up, then," said the carpenter, and they both bent their heads back, to examine the roof above them. High in the vaulted ceiling, the plaster was peeling and an area of black damp spread from one corner. "What's beyond the roof?"

"The sky."

"And what's beyond the sky?"

"Space. Planets. The stars."

"Exactly," breathed Mr. Butterfield. "It's been the same ever since people had eyes to look. Same constellations, same galaxies. But supposing one night you looked up and saw a new star . . ."

"A supernova, you mean?"

"Or a comet, or an intergalactic meteorite skipping over the earth's atmosphere — doesn't matter which. Just suppose this brand new twinkling pinpoint of light looked you in the eye . . . and *winked*."

The two uncricked their necks and stared at one another. And the carpenter began a new story . . .

———

Far away in the East, three astronomers uncricked their necks and stared at one another. "A new star? What does it mean?" said Caspar.

"An omen!" said Melchior, eyes full of starlight.

"Saddle the camels!" said Balthazar. "We must go and see for ourselves. Someone's been born who's going to change the history of the world!"

The three scholars took their bearings from the new star and traveled west. Their camels waded through rivers, struggled over sand dunes, spat at robbers lurking in the dark. During the day, the three sheltered from the sun and from sand-storms, biting mosquitoes, knife-edged winds. But every night they rode on, led by the star, clutching gifts for the newborn king. For surely, someone whose coming warranted a new star in the sky must be an emperor or a king.

Riding into Jerusalem at long last, they made for the palace, of course, and explained their mission to the king who lived there. "Where is the new king whose birth we have seen written in the stars?" they asked. "We've come a long way to pay our respects to him!"

King Herod only ruled in Israel by permission of the Romans. But he clung on grimly to his crown and his throne and his little bit of power. Now, a pang of anger went through him like an arrow; he knew of no such birth. New king? New king? he thought to himself. I am the only king of the Jews!

But to the three travelers he said, "I'm afraid I know nothing of this star-child. When you find him, please come back and tell me, so that I, too, may . . . pay my respects." Under the folds of his robe, his fingers toyed with a dagger in its jeweled sheath. These three scholars might be wise in the ways of the night sky, but Herod had cunning enough to snuff out that star of theirs . . .

"You'd need very long arms to snuff out a star," said the boy.

Mr. Butterfield nodded. "And Herod might have been a big, important man, but inwardly he was small-minded, and small-minded people never reach the stars."

Much to the astonishment of Caspar, Melchior, and Balthazar, the star finally came to rest over the small town of Bethlehem. The roads were so narrow that the camels had to move in single file. Somewhere a dog barked. The three wondered if they hadn't made some terrible mistake along the way. What an exotic sight they must have been for anyone out late that night: three men outlandishly dressed, gabbling in a foreign language and pointing at the stars. What strange noises the innkeeper and his customers must have heard as they turned over in their beds: camels groaning and belching and slumping down onto their knees.

What a strange night for Mary: three dust-stained, wealthy foreigners thrusting gifts at her and the baby. What a strange discovery for the astronomers: weary, working people, a baby in a feed box, the nervy animals stepping from hoof to hoof. And yet, for this moment, fire had kindled in the distant galaxies, and careered across the night sky to announce the birth of a king!

Mary took the presents: a bag of foreign gold, a box of frankincense. (She had smelled the scent before on the hair and clothes of cousin Zechariah after a day spent inside God's Temple.) Lastly, the visitors presented a jar of myrrh.

The chisel slipped, sinking its blade into the carpenter's left palm.

"You've hurt yourself!"

"It's nothing," said Mr. Butterfield. But blood welled up in the cut and fell onto his work — onto the half-carved manger. They both watched it redden the wood.

"An odd gift for a baby — myrrh," said Mr. Butterfield, licking his cut. "It's for the dead, you know. An ointment used to anoint dead people . . . But then that's why he came, you see? That little baby. Once he was grown up, Jesus did a lot of important things. But most important of them all was dying."

They both looked up at the stained-glass window above them: a green hill, a brown cross, a man who was Jesus, spilling his blood to wash away all the wrongs in the world.

"It's like you said once," Mr. Butterfield recalled. "Jesus was like the sheep who died in place of Isaac. He was like that offering on Elijah's altar. He was God's ultimate rescue plan!"

"He was like David slaying the big bad giant!"

"He was the way back to Paradise Garden!"

"He was the ram God gave to Abraham!"

Their hands brushed as they pointed to different symbols on the Jesse tree, remembering all the stories they had shared.

"He's Once-upon-a-time and The End!" said Mr. Butterfield.

They sat down breathless, their backs against the trunk of the Jesse tree.

"I'm sorry you hurt your hand."

"Don't worry about it, son. Tree's all but finished, isn't it? All but done. I'll mend, don't you fret. I'll mend. But speaking of blood . . . I haven't finished telling you about King Herod."

ANGELS

Mr. Butterfield groaned as he tried to make himself comfortable. Then he began.

Herod waited and waited, digging his dagger into the arm of his throne, ruining the gilded woodwork. Where were those three astronomers? As soon as they returned, he would know where to find that newborn king. He already knew how to stop it from ever stealing his crown . . . Tchk, tchk went the dagger's blade into the arm of his chair . . . Gathering up their memories, brushing the straw off their robes, Caspar, Melchior, and Balthazar camped outside Bethlehem and lay gazing up at the dancing constellations. Happy and weary, they quickly fell asleep.

Suddenly — soft as sheep's wool, white as sheet lightning — an angel came swooping into their dreams. "Don't go back to Jerusalem! Don't tell King Herod what he wants to know! He would kill the child, not worship at his cradle. Go home! Go home another way!"

So that's what they did, urging their camels into a gallop, cutting their pack mules loose. Caspar was in such a panic to obey the angel that he never stopped to wonder how he and Melchior and Balthazar had come to dream the same dream at the same moment. They simply fled, offering up prayers for that helpless little child, to the glittering, frosty stars.

The angel meanwhile turned back, flying through Bethlehem that night until he reached the sleeping Joseph. He had a second message, this time for the carpenter from Nazareth: "Get up, Joseph! You are not safe. King Herod wants the child dead. Make for Egypt, and stay there until the danger has passed!"

So that's what Joseph did. The sight probably didn't cause much of a stir: a little family with their donkey, crossing an unmarked border into the Egyptian wilderness. They glanced back from time to time for signs they were being followed, but mostly they looked ahead. Hanging from the saddle were a pot of gold, a box of incense, and a jar of myrrh. Cradled in Mary's arms was the Savior of the world.

They would get by, Joseph comforted himself. God would take care of everything . . . And anyway, a good carpenter can pick up work anywhere.

"You must carve an angel," said the boy.

"I don't know. There'll be a star — here — right at the very top."

"Oh, but you have to put in God's messenger. There, look. He'll just fit, if you carve him small."

"Very well. No one seems to know how big angels are. In fact philosophers have been arguing about it for years. Just here, do you mean? As if he's in the stable?"

"Well, of course he was. All the angels went along there after they left the shepherds. Millions of them! To take a look. Wouldn't you?"

If Mr. Butterfield wondered how anyone could be so sure, he was too busy to ask — too busy planning the final feature of his crowded Jesse tree.

THE BRIGHTEST STAR

"Finished!" Mr. Butterfield lifted the sandpaper from the star. "The brightest star," he said under his breath. "God's brightest star."

His work was finished, and it pleased him. The woodcarving flourished in the church now like a living tree, its branches crowded with animals, signs, and symbols. It was almost like a Christmas tree decked with ornaments, all rising towards the Christmas star. A year-round Christmas tree. A lifelong Christmas tree, you might almost say.

He wished the boy could see it. But the boy was gone. Either his vacation had ended or he had guessed the stories were at an end. "I could have always told him the other stories," said Mr. Butterfield sadly to himself. "There are so many . . ." But there would be no more wet dogs, no more little brothers, no more ice creams or awkward questions, no more demands to "Tell me!"

Mr. Butterfield had never thought he could miss anyone so much.

There again, lots of visitors came to the church, especially in the summer: plenty of tourists, dozens of children . . . The thought lifted his flagging spirits.

Tipping linseed oil into a rag, he began to polish: the sitting camel, Jacob's ladder, Joseph's sandals . . . It was only when he came to the angel — only as he oiled the outstretched arm, the little open hand, the bright smile — that he saw it. It gave his heart the oddest jolt.

For there was the boy's face! Without realizing it, he must have shaped the brow, the jaw, the lips and created a perfect likeness.

Tell me, the mouth seemed to say. Make me see!

Mr. Butterfield sat down at the foot of his Jesse tree. "Well, blow me down!" he whispered up at the glossy angel. "Who would've thought it?"

No, now he looked at it, the mouth was not asking for a story at all, but telling one. "Once upon a time . . ." To everyone who came now and stood looking with idle curiosity at the Jesse tree, wondering what stories hung ripening among its branches, this little face would speak.

If only they had the ears to listen.

"Go ahead, lad. It's your turn. Tell me. Make me see," said Mr. Butterfield to the angel. "I'm listening now."